That most holy and joyful of holidays, the day of goodwill towards men and the redemption of Ebenezer Scrooge and the Grinch and the television adventures of Rudolph and Hermey and Yukon Cornelius. It was songs and family and most of all (at least if you were one of the children in the town), the bright downtown lights and all the presents to follow. For even though they had a witch, this was a town that took its Christmases, and with them its Hanukkahs, very seriously indeed.

Also by Torger Vedeler

Intersect: A Love Story
Layers
Doughnuts of the Gods

The Christmas Witch

and Other Stories

Torger Vedeler

Altakkme Books

The Christmas Witch and Other Stories

ISBN: 978-1-936783-23-6 (paperback)
ISBN: 978-1-936783-24-3 (e-book)

Altakkme Books
altakkme@gmail.com

For Mama, Papa, Erik and Chris

and

Heather and Jasmine

Contents

The Christmas Witch

One

It was a long time ago, the children all say, that the old house became scary, a frightening place of mystery and gloom there at the end of the street. Cut off from its neighbors by a ragged wooden fence and two empty lots besides, by thick trees around the back, it loomed large in the mythology of the neighborhood and the town, a frightening story yet untold. Dark windows marked its face, and closed doors, the yard unkempt and overgrown by thorn and thistle. Two floors with a basement below and a small attic above, a pitched, shingled roof, unadorned siding. The windows that faced the street rarely showed more than drawn curtains, and who knew what lay behind the drapery? There was occasionally smoke from the chimney, no doubt from the simmering of some noxious brew, and the reputation of the place made it easy to ignore the modern utility meter on one wall, or even the fact that there was a small garage, unless, of course, this was where the Witch kept her flying broomsticks.

But really, this creepy reputation was hardly the fault of the children. Beginning very young they were always warned, "Stay away, stay away!" by parents and teachers, who watched the place and shook their heads and let these warnings take on a life of their own in young imaginations. "The old woman there is bad, she is mean, she is cruel!" the children then told one another. "She'll gobble you up, an old hag with a wart on her nose, will boil you into stew, or she will chase you into darkness and you will never return!"

Now, none of this is to say that the Witch never emerged from her dark abode. There she was sometimes, a cane in her left hand, her shoes making a click click click sound as she walked over the sidewalk, her gaze straight ahead, never looking at you, never seeming to notice that you were even there. Down the short street from her dark house, to turn left and make her way, people parting before her like the Red Sea before Moses.

Click... click... click....

Occasionally she went to the cemetery, and for the children and more than a few adults this too was clear proof of her witchcraft. She would go to a particular grave and there stand before it, sometimes muttering quietly to herself. What she muttered was never really clear, for no one ever wanted to get close enough to listen. This too must be dark magic, they said, and although the gravestone was well tended and never bereft of flowers, it too was still probably cursed.

And of course, even witches must eat, so you would occasionally see her at the store with her little cart for groceries, buying oatmeal (we all know that unsweetened oatmeal is a favorite food of witches), and sometimes she went downtown, to the bank, because likewise it is common knowledge that witches hoard gold coins. So when she did emerge from her dark and weathered home the townspeople would stare, drawing their children back and whispering amongst themselves after she had gone out of earshot, adding rumor to speculation and turning this into myth.

"How old is she?"

"No one knows. She came here from outside."

"Outside?"

"Some other town. I never heard which one. Probably out of state, though. Came with Omar MacCamey when he got back, I heard. They were already married."

"And?"

A shrug. "Like I said, no one's sure. Omar never said much about what he did those years he was away, but I heard he made money, a lot of money."

"And then he died and she got it all?" Eyes would narrow. "Sounds suspicious."

"They said it was a stroke that killed him, but he was only in his forties, which is awfully young."

"Black widow?"

"I'm not saying. But look how she dresses."

A frown, maybe a scowl.

"Well, if you're really so curious about her, you could always ask Mr. Handell. He handled Omar MacCamey's will."

But the lawyer and banker Mr. Handell (that's two Ls at the end, by the way, not one like the composer, and yes, I am aware of the verbal pun in the sentence above), never said anything about the Witch's business with him, which was proper, after all, and it is important that you all know that Mr. Handell was a very proper man. He had that tall and professional bearing of his trade, always in a suit and tie, smiling on occasion only, the books in all accounts neatly kept. This brought him affection and quiet admiration from the townspeople, who knew that their money was safe with him, in any event, and so whatever he might know about the Witch, they were content to let him keep it to himself.

And so it was, one year and then another and another, Halloweens in succession, until children she had frightened became adults with children of their own, still watching her, still whispering and wondering if she had always been this old, if as a witch she could age at all.

The Witch, the Crone, the Hag.

* * *

But let us put Halloween aside (however appropriate it might feel), since it was easy to ignore the old house and the Witch on that creepy late October night and seek your treats at other, more promising homes. These would have plastic skeletons and glowing, false-scary lights to mark them, and you went out secure in the knowledge that it was really only Mr. Snead or Mr. Bechhoefer shaking the tree branches for a goodnatured laugh, or Mr. Cisneros commenting after mock alarm on the cleverness of your costume, each then to distribute the expected reward of candy and treats.

But Christmas? Ah, Christmas was something more, something special indeed in the small town. That most holy and joyful of holidays, the day of goodwill towards men and the redemption of Ebenezer Scrooge and the Grinch and the television adventures of Rudolph and Hermey and Yukon Cornelius. It was songs and family and most of all (at least if you were one of the children in the town), the bright downtown lights and all the presents to follow. For even though they had a witch, this was a town that took its Christmases, and with them its Hanukkahs, very seriously indeed.

Why this was no one really knows, but just as with the lawyer and banker Mr. Handell it is important for our tale that you understand that it was so. And of all the people of the small town, no one took the obligation to celebrate Christmas more seriously, or with more vigor and zest, than Jip A. Batton III. If by circumstance or even simple forgetfulness you neglected your holiday duty, if your storefront was not awash with color and decoration, if you did not join in the singing of carols and act to spread the holiday spirit far and wide, there was always Jip A. Batton III on hand to remind you to do so.

Jip, you see, was everything the Witch was not. A vocal, public, gregarious man, he came from an old-money family that had settled in town as its summer home more than a century before and taken a liking to the place; his grandfather and father and an uncle had each been mayor (the uncle twice), and his home was that big one so hard to miss in the best neighborhood. He had patrician roots here, and he was proud of them.

More than any of this, however, Jip *loved* Christmas, adored everything about it, and like so many of us, his affection for the holiday was presumably based on fond childhood memories. What a wondrous time that must have been in the old Batton household, people said, as every year they witnessed Jip's passion for the tinsel and the ribbons and the happy songs. As early as August he would already be planning the festivities and charitable fundraisers, meeting with the town council and assuring them that this year's celebration would be better than the last, that there would be *more* lights downtown and *more* displays in the store windows, and a longer line of children for Santa than ever before. Santa himself was selected with care, auditioned for belly and "Ho! Ho! Ho!" by Jip himself. Indeed, if he saw you and thought you qualified, you can be sure he would call until you agreed to come in for a jolly audition, because nothing was too good for Christmas, nothing at all.

This great effort eventually paid great dividends, and with time the town's holiday reputation spread. In December people would come from cities all around and they would remark at the spirit of Christmas here, lining up to shake Jip's hand and praise him for the effort.

"It's nothing, really," he always said. "You're too kind. Merry Christmas!"

But there *was* still the Witch, and it didn't take long for Jip to notice the empty space among the neighborhood decorations. Every year he would drive by and look at the dark, solemn house and shake his head, a frown crossing his features, because every year this was the single place where there were no lights, where there was no joy, where the spirit of Christmas seemed conspicuously so absent.

"Isn't there some way we can get her on board?" he asked the town council one year after a fruitless effort of knocking on the Witch's front door three times in four days. "Maybe an ordinance we can invoke? What does it say about us, that this one person can just ignore the holiday?" He looked at the men and women of the council. "Just look at that place she lives in! It's a wreck! Is her home even up to the fire code?"

"It is," said the fire chief, whose name was Mr. Byczkiewicz. "The roof was replaced only five years ago, and the boards on her walls the year before that, even if she didn't come out while they worked; her accountant Mr. Handell handled everything. So maybe it's not pretty, but her house is livable and safe. She isn't breaking any laws."

"Well," said Jip again. "It just isn't right, not celebrating either Christmas or at least

Hanukkah. It's just not neighborly. Something should be done." And he sat down with a frown as they began to debate the endless and unfathomable excitement of zoning ordinances.

Now, say what you will, dear reader, but no one could ever accuse Jip Batton of giving up easily. He thought about the silent, dark house for a long time, and when a few years later he came up with his answer and a scheme to go along with it, it just happened to be the same chilly autumn that young Betsy Shore knocked the old witch down.

Two

Now, young Betsy Shore was certainly more than four (rendering such a Dr. Seuss rhyme about her quite unworkable), but do not forget that she was no adult either. Instead we may say that Betsy lay at that awkward age when the magic of childhood is beginning to yield to the harder truths of adolescence, to responsibility and maybe a little rebellion, though not there yet. Whether she actually believed in Santa Claus not even she could really say, but like everybody else in town she *was* certain about the Witch. Betsy's home, after all, sat just down the street from the ancient, scary house, and Betsy's parents had always reminded her to leave the old woman alone, not to go "over there," a lesson easy to instill in a child when the place looked like it did.

And Betsy did love Christmas. After all, like the other children of the town, our not-so-little-anymore Betsy had grown up with the dazzle of Jip Batton's Christmas lights, with parades and storefronts and gifts with ribbons. She, like all of us, had heard again and again the ten sacred, dishonest, and unachievable words of American retail, amplified into a frenzy for the holiday: *The Customer is Always Right* and *You Get Something for Nothing.* And more than these there had been the chants and songs everyone sang beneath them, or loudly broadcast on radio and television and the internet and street-corners everywhere, easy to distill in the joy and excitement of the season.

> *Shop! Shop! Shop shop shop! Christmas love is found in a package with bows!*

How many times had she rushed downstairs on Christmas morning to find her stocking full of treats? How many trees in the living room, shining with decorations and surrounded by bright boxes of joyous mystery? From the lists of desires she and her siblings made every year to the trips to the mall to point those desires out, surely the season was a wonder.

Ah, but *our* story is about the Witch, isn't it, and so let us return to her. It began with something small, you know. Just a little thing, almost nothing at all. Shopping for groceries one autumn day, the aisles busy, children squawking to mothers and fathers, infants screaming and testing patience, while overworked and underpaid retail clerks labored at the registers or stocked shelves, some of them trying to explain to impatient consumers that sometimes advertised things just run out of stock, that this is not the end of the world and is nobody's fault (least of all theirs), the mayhem of a Saturday afternoon a week and a half before Thanksgiving. And there was Betsy, rushing through, in the kind of hurry only a young girl can achieve, around a corner, looking back instead of forward.

Ter-Clunk!

The basket falls, cans and little bags scatter. A crown of broccoli here, a box of teabags there. And when not-so-little-anymore Betsy looks up, only the sudden silence greets her, for there, sprawled on the floor, was the Witch.

Betsy's first instinct, the logical, reasonable instinct hammered into her through years of warnings and stories of children boiling in pots, was to run. Perhaps, in fact, had they been outside, had there not been people all around blocking the way, she would have. But it was too crowded with shoppers and carts and an employee or two, so there was no escape for our poor, young Betsy. Instead those critical seconds passed and she simply stared at the fallen woman, jaw agape.

What do you see, young Betsy?

The Witch! The old hag, with a crooked nose and a malevolent stare, the subject of a lifetime of warnings?

Or?

What do *you* see, gentle reader? What do any of us ever really want to see? What do we

16

choose, when we pass another? How do we judge?

How are *we* judged?

And this is, perhaps, the most remarkable thing of all. Betsy stared at the Witch, gawking for those crucial few seconds, and then she got up. She got up and she stepped to the old woman, words coming from her mouth that would have been inconceivable even a minute before.

"Oh! I'm so sorry! Are you okay?"

No one moved as the Witch looked back at her. Perhaps they awaited a curse, a bitter tirade about the clumsiness of youth. Perhaps even a magic spell. But instead there were only words, in a voice raspy from disuse.

"I... think so."

Mr. Zorn, herding his own two small children, acted then, joined by Ms. Macpherson and then Walter the clerk, who had been stocking beans. They abandoned their carts and stepped forward. They helped the Witch to her feet, and Betsy began to pick up the mess. A bottle had broken, leaving a stain of strawberry jam on the floor, mixed in now with shards of glass that rendered it quite inedible. And when

Betsy saw this, she said something more without thinking, something that would change
everything forever.

"Let me get you another one."

The Witch looked at her and Betsy froze,
still expecting a snarl, a curse, maybe a cruel
word. But instead there, to Betsy and
everyone else's surprise, only a shy smile.

"Thank you."

* * *

News got out, and in time it got to Jip
Batton. He was sitting in his office when it did,
well-immersed in planning and organizing with
only a little more than a month to go before
Christmas Eve. As always, he was excited,
humming carols in anticipation, checking every
detail. It would be bigger this year, better, and
of course there would be all those people
wanting to talk to him about all that he had
done; he even had a new necktie picked out
with Santa and the reindeer soaring through the
night.

"Did you hear?" his secretary asked.

"Hear what?"

"The Witch. There's quite a buzz. A little girl knocked her down at the store. I heard about it from Ms. Laidlaw, who heard it from Mr. Beverage in his office, who I think heard it from someone who was there. Knocked the old hag right down and toppled a display, maybe two! That poor kid!"

Now, as I mentioned before, it would be untrue to say that Jip had forgotten about the Witch. Indeed, she and her holiday isolation had been more and more on his mind this year, so since his latest drive by her dim and dismal house, an idea began to brew in his head, one, he thought, that might just work. He turned from his computer.

"Tell me more."

These are always dangerous words, because for many of us (your humble narrator sometimes included, I'm afraid) it is the *talking* that matters, not what is *said.* And when two or three or four people talk who know little, it is a natural human failing for each to start embellishing, claiming that we know more than we actually do, so soon enough it is the story, not the events, that really matters. In this case, when the story was over at last, poor Jip knew only but with great certainty that the Witch had shouted at the innocent girl and waved her gnarled cane at her, and that at least a hundred people had seen her do it, and then the old woman had left the store with threats of lawsuits and other needless mischief.

This, he told himself with a confident and self-directed nod, is what comes from not celebrating Christmas.

Meanwhile, as rumors spread like bubbles forming in an overheated cauldron, Betsy walked the Witch home, helping carry her groceries. We do not know, and nor did she, just why she did this. Maybe it was a sense of obligation for her carelessness, wanting to make sure the old woman was really all right, or maybe it was curiosity (this *was* the Witch, after all), or maybe, just maybe, Betsy was seeing something in the hag that no one else in town had ever seen before. But whatever the reason, the two of them got to the old house and up to the front door, and there the Witch opened it and turned to the girl.

A quiet smile, almost shy, crossed her wrinkled face.

"Thank you," she said.

"It's all right," Betsy answered, and then she added, "I live right over there."

"I know," said the Witch.

"You do?"

"You and your sister and brother sometimes play in the front."

It had never occurred to Betsy, just as it too seldom occurs to any of us, that those we might watch could be watching us as well. And if the Witch's voice was quiet (and it was), that did not mean she was silent.

Quiet and hidden but suddenly real. Her eyes on the old woman, Betsy spoke again.

"If you need anything…."

The Witch reached out and touched Betsy's hand. Her fingers were warm, and she nodded.

"Thank you."

As she turned to cross the street for home, Betsy wondered if she had actually seen a tear forming in the old woman's eye.

Preposterous! the old voices said. *Witches never weep.*

Three

Since at least the time of the ancient Persian Empire, delivering mail has been an honorable, noble profession, and so it remains today. Thus the envelope from the town hall made its way quickly through the sorters and the machines and into the hands of Ms. Whitmore the local carrier, who it must be said had no fear of either dogs or witches, and from her satchel into the mailbox of the tired old house at the end of the street.

It held a summons, complete with a date and a time to appear next week, and there you were directed to explain just what you were going to do about the unkempt mess of bushes and wretched shrubs before your house. There have been complaints, you see, that these are an eyesore, and so we need an explanation and a solution, posthaste.

Such a thing will not do, not in our nice little town, not at all.

And so on the first day of December, the old Witch put on her best black dress and took her cane and her purse (yes, some witches carry purses; didn't you know?), and went in her shoes that went click click click down to the town hall, where the assembled town council awaited her as the fifth little thing they had on the agenda today, that she do as they asked and explain herself.

They read her name and she nodded. The room was all but empty save for her and the council members, most people having much better things to do on a late autumn day than to watch a tired town council scold an old woman.

The lone exception to this was Jip Batton, who stood at the back where observers normally would, watching and waiting, his eyes moving back and forth between them.

"There has been a complaint," said the mayor, half-bored but perhaps fascinated as well, for how often do you really get to see a witch? "Your front yard is a mess and needs to have the brush cleared. I see also that you own the two lots adjacent; these need to have the brush cleared as well. Is there a reason this has not been done?"

The Witch said nothing for a moment, and it would not be too much to wonder if she was assembling the words for an evil spell, some abra-kadabra-bumbilly-boo that would turn the council into ugly frogs or some other such a thing. But when she did speak her voice emerged soft, and had the room not been so quiet, no one would have heard her at all.

"No. I'm sorry."

Expecting an argument and getting none, the mayor fidgeted for a moment, twiddling with his pen.

"So you'll clean it up?" he asked.

Another pause.

"Yes."

No curse? No scowl? No threats of a pox upon the council members and their families for a dozen generations? This was proving to be quite the anticlimax.

"Very good," said the mayor, and that was all.

Almost.

As the Witch left the council chamber, Jip fell into step beside her and introduced himself.

"You probably know of me," he said, giving her his most charming smile. "I'm responsible for a lot of things around here, but especially the Christmas celebrations and charities."

The Witch didn't answer right away. Then she said, "Yes."

"Well, that's fine. And I have heard so much about you, though I didn't know you also owned those two empty lots beside your house. That's a good neighborhood. Good investments."

The Witch said nothing, still walking. Jip cleared his throat to fill the silence.

"Anyhow," he went on, "since I'm in charge of the town's Christmas decorations this year, I wanted to ask what you planned on doing with your house. It would look wonderful with lights. And those two lots have some lovely trees that could be decorated…."

It's an old trick of the salesman: Start the conversation as though the sale is already made. People hate to say no, after all. They hate to hurt your feelings or to disappoint, and once you see this, it's time for the closer, time to get them to sign on the dotted line and to whip out their wallets. But the Witch still said nothing, and now they were at the front doors. Jip tried flattery.

"Your home is quite lovely, you know. It'll look fantastic with Christmas lights. It wouldn't be any trouble, either. I'll find you some people you could hire to do the work." He gave her his charming smile once again. "You wouldn't have to get your hands dirty."

Now, keep in mind that Jip was an intelligent man, and he did pride himself with good reason at being able to read people. But he didn't see the Witch tense, her shoulders drawing just a little tight. Perhaps this was because he was confidently waiting for her reply, though this didn't come.

"So we can count on you this year?" he asked finally.

She didn't look at him, didn't turn. But she did give him an answer.

"No."

In every culture, in every society, there are certain words and things that at certain times are considered forbidden. They break an unwritten rule, maybe many, and those who state them or do them are quickly outcast. So it is especially at Christmas, and so especially it is for the most obviously and publicly charitable, those like Jip Batton. He stopped and stared at the Witch, and maybe, just maybe, if he had been thinking, if he had been more accustomed to people telling him "no," he would not have said what he then said. But that's the thing about words, why we should all be more careful with them: Once they are spoken, they cannot be unspoken.

"You're disgusting," he told her.

She froze for a few seconds, watching him. Perhaps she was surprised, and certainly rendered speechless. But Jip met her stare, his eyes angry, met it and held it until she trembled and looked away, until she stepped back and walked off quickly, hurrying back to the sanctuary of her worn and disheveled home.

* * *

For at least a day the Witch's house was dark and silent, and what scheming might have been going on inside must remain a mystery. Jip also was quiet, in his case more publicly so, lost in thought sitting at his desk, and likewise we do not know what thoughts he might have had. But eventually he returned to work, making phone calls and meeting with his sources, determined now that *this* Christmas the celebrations would be even grander than ever before, with more lights and more trees and more singing, impossible for even an old hag in her dark home to ignore.

And then the Witch emerged, venturing out into a cold autumn day to take the short walk past her empty side lot and to the house beyond, the house of the family of Betsy Shore. She did this in the afternoon, after school was over, after Betsy had returned.

The Witch rang the doorbell.

We can only wonder how this story might have gone had Betsy herself not answered, if instead it had been a parent or a sibling. History is often made from such small coincidences, you know, the importance of which become clear only later. But Betsy did answer the door, and there stood the Witch.

"Oh, hello," Betsy said, more than a little surprised.

The Witch managed a small, shy smile, her gaze down.

"Hello. I hope… I'm not intruding."

For Betsy it was a chance to put off homework. "Oh, no," she said. "It's fine." And then her manners caught up with her. "Would you like to come in?"

The Witch paled. "Can we walk instead?" she asked.

"Okay."

They stepped outside, the few feet to the fence between Betsy's home and the empty lot. The Witch was quiet until they arrived.

"They want me to clean it up," she said then, and indicated the brush, her voice soft with embarrassment. "I could hire someone, but I thought…. Would you like to do it? I can pay you."

Betsy looked at the lot, at the overgrown tangles, at the fence. Then she looked at the old woman and she remembered the scattered groceries, the broken jar of jam, and she said the first thing that came into her head.

"Sure."

Such a girl Betsy was! But she was also only one girl, and although she had all the energy of youth, it's hard to imagine how she could possibly have cleared all those years of neglected growth by herself. But it is wise never to underestimate how clever a girl can be, and so after one afternoon working alone, she returned the next day with friends.

Twila, Denise, Liz, (whose friends affectionately called her "the Lizard"), Billy, Robert (dubbed "Don Roberto" by *his* friends), Gene, Jon, Marty (who had the odd nickname "Share-sharrum"), and Daniel. All came, first with bare hands and then with gloves and tools borrowed from their parents' garages. And if they first came out of curiosity about the infamous and mysterious Witch, we must say that they also came with an ethic of hard work that would make any adult proud. And as one day became another and the weekend arrived, the street was filled with their laughter and good-natured fun, because it is a fact well known that hard work is always easier when you can share a chuckle and a joke with a friend.

They didn't see the Witch, who remained inside her dark house with the curtains still drawn, but every time they arrived there would be a table outside with cookies and drinks and a card that said "Thank You" together with an envelope for Betsy that held twenty-dollar bills and a note to share these with her friends. And as they took these the kids began to remark among themselves about their mysterious em-ployer.

"What does she look like?" they asked Betsy.

The girl shrugged. "An old lady, I guess."

One of them thought about asking whether she had a wart on her nose, but thought better of this and didn't.

"Why doesn't she come out?" someone did ask.

"Maybe she's shy."

They all agreed that this was possible, and remarkably, that it was also perfectly all right. They all knew shy kids at school, after all, and some of them were a little shy themselves. Nothing wrong with that. And more than one of them thought about the things they had always heard about the Witch, the scary stories and warnings, and more than one began to wonder if maybe, just maybe, all those things they had always heard weren't actually true.

They were *really* good cookies, after all, fresh baked and homemade, with no witch's poison or anything.

Four

So as December marched steadily on towards Christmas, the Witch was seeming less witchy, and her yard less cluttered and now a place of innocent, youthful laughter, this fueled by the cookies and the end of school for the holiday break. Then, on one of these days a long and formal car appeared and parked out front, and from this long and formal car emerged the tall and distinguished Mr. Handell in his suit and tie, carrying his attaché case. He regarded the youngsters and gave them an approving nod before walking right up to the front door, where he rang the bell. The door opened and he went inside, and that was that until he emerged more than two hours later as the sun was going down and the busy teenagers were finishing their last treats and waiting for rides home, Betsy waiting with them before making the short walk home herself.

Of course, when the teenagers got home they mentioned all this to their parents, who mentioned it to friends the next day, and eventually word got to Jip, as it always did. So the morning after that he appeared at Mr. Handell's office.

"May I have a word?" he asked.

Ever polite, Mr. Handell asked him in.

"What can I do for you, Mr. Batton?"

"You were at Mrs. MacCamey's house a few days ago, I'm told," Jip said.

Mr. Handell raised a single brow. "Yes."

"You handle her affairs, I'm told."

To this Mr. Handell was silent. Jip cleared his throat and went on.

"She has, I'm sure, money. Maybe a great deal of money, I hear, from her late husband. And I have it on good authority that she is a miser."

Look now at Mr. Handell's face. Expressionless, perhaps too much so. He leaned forward just a bit.

"Now Jip," he said, "you know as well as I do that I cannot talk about that sort of thing. Financial matters are confidential."

To say nothing, of course, is to let another say anything. What Jip had suspected he now felt was confirmed. The old woman not only refused to celebrate the holiday, but she *was* a miser, a cheapskate, an unredeemed Scrooge, or Scroogess, if you prefer. She deserved no mercy.

"I have it on good authority that she's exploiting those children," he said. "Doesn't that bother you?"

There are those in the world who can be bullied, who you can sway with clever arguments and rhetoric and even veiled threats, who are taught from early on to avoid conflict at all costs and so too easily give in. But there are also those whom you cannot so sway, who recognize manipulation immediately and have no tolerance for it. Mr. Handell regarded Jip, and he spoke clearly.

"Mr. Batton," he said in his most formal tone, "I appreciate your coming by, but you will be happy to hear that there is no cause for concern. I saw the children at work at her house, work which she is having done at your insistence, if I am not mistaken, since I know it was you who complained to the town council about her yard. The children I saw working there seemed both happy and are well compensated. I would say that to do such work is good for them, as it helps to build character. Now, Christmas is only about a week away and I'm sure you have many things to attend to. Let Mrs. MacCamey keep the holiday in her own way, as you keep it in yours. One house without holiday lights is hardly a catastrophe."

Not yet, anyway.

* * *

They finished working on December 23, feeling perhaps a bit sad that there was no more, and thus no more of the delicious cookies and fun of a hard task shared among friends. But the holiday was close, and all of them had families to join and Christmas or Hanukkah or other celebrations to attend, and so they collected their last envelopes from Betsy and smiled at the colorful cards and extra bills within, looking up at the cloudy sky which, the meteorologist predicted, might just bring a snowstorm.

At about this same time the news truck arrived from the big city, carrying with it a camerawoman named Sonya, a lighting specialist named Bobbi, the expert technical support team of Ed and Ted, and of course Ms. Molly Kilczer, television personality and reporter extraordinaire, here to tape their Christmas special report from the town now famous for its decorations and celebration.

Jip, of course, was the first to be interviewed, and gave the longest response, going into great detail.

"We're all very pleased with our effort this year," he told the reporter. "I managed to get extra lighting on Main Street, and because I know someone who has a tree farm, we got the biggest tree we've ever had. I got extra lights and decorations donated, and we've also put a big menorah beside it. I'm especially proud of that, since it's new this year. The whole town is alight with the holiday spirit! Oh, and our charity fundraiser went very well also."

"How long have you been doing this?" asked the industrious Ms. Kilczer.

"I've been in charge for almost twenty years, Molly. It's a huge honor for me, every year, and every year I dare say we have the most Christmas spirit ever!"

He let them go finally with a smile and a photo-op, but the crew didn't return to the big city right away. Molly made sure they got footage of all the decorations, and then she and her crew went out into the town to gather some local color and talk to some local citizens. This took longer than they thought it would, and when they returned to the big city the snow had begun to fall more heavily.

Five

Christmas Eve dawned with snow still coming down and a good six inches on the ground. The storm passed a little after noon, by which time excited children were already out playing, tossing snowballs and building snowmen and snowwomen and the occasional snow space alien with sticks for antennae, while trucks with plows and salt worked the streets, bringing their drivers some welcome extra income. Bells rang in churches and many people gathered for worship and to provide charity for those less fortunate, while others cuddled around fireplaces at home, looking at their own trees and decorations and preparing their Christmas Eve dinners, maybe sharing some bubbly juice or Norwegian gjetost or chocolates sent by loved ones far away. Phone calls were made and cards opened, smiles moving across faces at the reminders of kindness. For each family and person had their own customs and traditions, their own ways to celebrate, even as all looked forward to the early darkness, when the big lights downtown would come on.

Jip poured himself a glass of wine and settled in front of the television. As always, it was set to record the news, but he also enjoyed watching it live, to hear the inevitable praise from the news anchors, the sight of all his hard work getting the recognition it deserved. Every year better than the last, he told himself, and by watching these reports he could pick out things to make even bigger and more colorful for next year.

The interview went well. He had on his Christmas tie, of course, and had made certain that his hair was newly and professionally cut. A little Christmas tree pin adorned his lapel, and his smile was, as always, smooth and charming. The lighting tech had done a good job, and he sounded good, too.

Molly spoke. "The man chiefly responsible for all these decorations is Jip Batton, who has been doing this for many years now. Mr. Batton, what inspired you to start this tradition?"

"Well, it *is* Christmas, Molly. I like to give back."

Perfect, with his best and most charming smile. Smooth and polished. He wondered how many people were watching.

Then the scene changed.

Ms. Molly Kilczer, television personality and reporter extraordinaire, standing on a different street, in front of an unlit house.

"But not all of the holiday need be celebrated with flashing lights and decorations," she said. "For others, there are simpler ways. As we visited this charming little town, we kept hearing stories of another act of holiday spirit, one we simply had to investigate. I'm standing at the home of an elderly resident where the yard outside has been cleaned up by a group of local schoolchildren. I have one of them here, a Ms. Betsy Shore. Why have you and your friends done this, Betsy?"

A shy, yet excited smile, because it was *television,* after all. "She's our neighbor," Betsy said. "She's a nice lady."

The camera showed the house, looking lovely indeed as the first snowflakes fell. Molly spoke again to the camera.

"We tried to reach Mrs. MacCamey, but since we're only here for a few hours, we weren't able to. Still, in this reporter's opinion, seeing her house cleaned up through the kindness of these children is an example of the very best of the holiday spirit. Thank you, Betsy. We're all very proud of you."

"Merry Christmas!" Betsy said.

And that was that, on to other news.

A good rage starts slow, before you are even aware it has begun. Some minor thing at first, nothing really, but like a pebble in your shoe it just won't go away, seeming to grow bigger with every step. It's not like a flash of sudden anger (which may bring its own disaster), but instead one where your inner voice keeps telling you to act, to react, to make right this wrong by any means you can.

This was the kind of fury that began to grow inside Jip Batton. It had, we must admit, been building for some time; weeks, certainly, but really years, every time he thought of the dark house and the old hag within, every holiday season when she would not celebrate as she should. That was bad enough, but to see her dark home *praised?* To see it *praised* in a news story that was supposed to be about *him?*

A news story that *everyone saw?*

His glass of wine was quickly drained, graduating to more than one shot of harder drink. Outside, the afternoon of Christmas Eve was fading into the Eve itself, and Jip knew that he would be expected downtown, to shake hands with the mayor and make his customary speech, to wish the townsfolk well. But did they deserve this? Who among them had ever done more for Christmas than he had? And who among them had told the reporter about Betsy Shore? Who had told the reporter about the old crone in her ugly house?

You have to go, he told himself. People have to see you. They have to notice you.

Another glass and then another, to warm him up and get him ready, until finally Jip Batton got into his car and drove off to meet his destiny.

* * *

You could see the stars now, sharp against the night's bitter cold and the snow freshly plowed from sidewalks around the town hall. The crowd, undeterred by the chill, began to gather, children bundled beneath layers of down and wool, the air cloudy with exhaled breath. Hands held hands and when someone began to sing others joined in, the old words coming naturally.

Oh, holy night,
The stars are brightly shining.

It is the night of our dear savior's birth.
Long lay the world in sin and error, pining,
'Til he appears and the soul felt its worth....

Perhaps, in the chill, someone noticed that Jip wore no hat and that his coat was unzipped. Perhaps someone saw his face and wondered that his expression looked a little off, that his eyes bore an unfamiliar darkness, that his cheeks seemed flush. Perhaps.

But this was Jip Batton, who they all thought they knew, whose family had come to town so many decades ago and established itself here, who lived in one of the finest houses in town and was a pillar of the community. The mayor shook his hand, and people applauded and cheered, the sounds muffled a bit by mittens and scarves.

Did the mayor see Jip teeter slightly as he stepped to the microphone?

Too late.

"Good evening! Merry Christmas!" Jip said.

A cheer. Hurrah!

"Look at this tree! It's the biggest one we've ever had!"

Another cheer.

"It took a lot of work for me to get this tree! I had to call in favors! I had to raise the money! How many of *you* gave?"

Do you hear it now? That little hesitation, that tiny delay? Mrs. Carmona glanced at her wife and a short way away Dr. Stewart raised a brow, like many others suddenly a little confused.

"How many years have I been doing this?" Jip roared. "What would Christmas be without *me?*"

Look there, gentle reader. Betsy Shore is standing, watching, holding her father's hand. Look at her eyes as they glance around. What does she see, our young Betsy?

"And then *she* gets all the credit!" Jip shouted. "Just for sitting in her ugly house and neglecting her lawn! I do *all* this, and the only thing they can talk about is *her,* the old witch!"

The crowd went silent, just staring. Betsy pressed close to her father. And right then, now realizing that something was very, very wrong, the mayor stepped over to Jip and gently tried to pull him away from the microphone, perhaps now smelling the liquor on his breath. To one side, the fire chief signaled the technician to cut the power to the PA system.

Not that it mattered. Jip was not finished yet.

"How is that fair?"

He was yelling now, the microphone and PA unnecessary. He shoved the mayor away.

"How is that fair? I gave you people the best Christmas you've ever had and all you can do is talk about the Witch and her goddamn ugly house!"

They made one last attempt to intervene, the police chief joining in, but alcohol and fury make for a potent combination and Jip pushed them aside, storming from the podium and through the shocked, parting crowd, away from them all and back to his car, starting the engine with a roar and driving off.

Of them all, it was Betsy who somehow knew where he was going. She pulled at her father's arm and in an urgent voice told him:

"We have to get home."

He heard the tone and nodded. Her mother and siblings heard it too and did not protest, all five of them hurrying back toward their own car. But this would take a few minutes because they had parked some distance away, and the delay brought Jip the time he needed.

The old house, pretty in snow, with trees and a newly cleared lawn in front, the street freshly plowed. A light on inside, warm and quiet.

And then, Jip's big car, weaving up the street, coming to a crunch against a bank of snowfall. The door opened, headlights illuminating the old house, and Jip emerged.

"You old hag!" he shouted.

The dark house, only one window alight, stared back at him.

"I gave you every chance! You could have joined us every year! But you *hate* Christmas, don't you? You hate everything about it! You make me sick!"

Still nothing. A wise man once said, only half in jest, that the only thing worse than to be hated is to be ignored. Perhaps this is so; I leave that for you to decide. I can only recount that Jip Batton looked around, and he saw that the plow had exposed some rocks beneath the new snowfall. Now he went to these, stumbling as he did, and picked one up.

"You witch! Get out here!"

Maybe it wasn't the first stone, but he cast it anyway.

Six

The rock shattered glass, this exploding inward and scattering, and it caught the point between curtains, penetrating deep to the table just beyond. On this table the Witch kept several framed photographs, and the stone knocked some of these over and to the floor.

Wait now and know this: A picture, a photograph or a painting, is more than simply an image, is more than mere pigment or emulsion or pixel. It is a reflection, a glimpse into a moment, an instant in time. And so it is also a part of memory, and as such, it is a part of *you*, both who you were and who you are.

Jip's stone impacted these, most importantly the one of a young man dressed in his finest, bearing a wide and loving smile, beside a young woman dressed in white with lace and satin and a bridal veil drawn back over her head, her own smile shy and tentative but also very real. This picture went over the side of the bureau, and it fell to the floor with the others, cracking the frame.

The Witch likewise fell, not from any blow, but from sudden fear, and seeing the picture hit the floor, she crawled quickly to it, even as the voice outside sounded again.

"I said get out here!"

Get. Out. Here.

Do you remember?

When you were a little girl, drawn back, holding your knees close to your chest. Voices. Not just one but many, scolding, stern. Those behind them wondering, maybe, what is wrong with you, wondering why their little daughter can't be like her sisters and brothers, why she so seldom speaks, why her teachers keep saying that she cannot learn, why she embarrasses everyone and is just not normal. No words for it, not in a culture where children should simply obey, should simply grow up right.

What is *wrong* with you?

But it is not all pain; remember that. Because there *are* her brothers and sisters, sometimes intervening to try and protect her, because they do love her even if she embarrasses them, even if she is strange. And her mother and her father are not evil either; they love her as only a parent can but they just don't know what to do, fearing for her future in a world where to be different too often means to be locked away forever.

Get. Out. Here.

She does grow, gets bigger, maybe pretty but never beautiful, not to most. School and grades and after much struggle a graduation, a young woman now who still seldom speaks, who becomes easy to ignore. But remember that just because you are ignored does not mean you ignore others in return. It does not mean you are nothing or that you are stupid, and it does not mean you will be forever forgotten.

A young man, maybe not the most handsome or athletic, but whip smart, the kind who sees things others miss. His full name was Omar Edward MacCamey and he fell in love with her because he could see where a thing or an idea or a person will be decades from today, could see who she was beyond the shy girl who was afraid of crowds. Instead he saw that she sees more deeply, past the superficial things we are all told to watch, and so one day he asked her her name and then he asked her to join him for a quiet walk. And he discovered, this Omar Edward MacCamey did, that for those with the patience to listen, she had a lot of wise things to say.

Wedding bells in a small chapel and her hand in his, the long white gloves to her elbows and the sound of the organ and the smile on the pastor's face as she whispers "I do" and so does he.

All this. Do you see it, when you see her? Do you wonder who she is when you decide who she is, knowing so little?

The voice outside was angry, lubricated by alcohol.

"You witch! You think I don't know what you did? You think I don't know what you are?"

They were the good years. With your husband, happy, the feel of his hand in yours and his kiss on your lips, the special way he said "I love you" and smiled when he saw you. And clever, too, both of you. Living simply, saving their money and buying a home and some land and making investments, seeing what could be and what would be and then, miraculous, unexpected success. Money, far more than the two of them ever imagined, because as brilliant as Omar was at making it, she had insight into what would someday be valuable, and they both had luck; they chose the shares of some companies that became great, that would change the world. And as she lay with him they both knew that this good fortune had brought them far more than they would ever need.

"We should give back," she tells him. "There are so many who could use a hand."

"Yes," he says.

But there is a danger, too, for what does wealth do to you? What does it do, when everyone knows you gave, when everyone knows you had enough to be so generous? Does the giving become about answering a need, or about yourself, your pride, your vanity? She asks Omar this and he nods, and they think about it. They ask their friend, the young Mr. Handell, who is just getting started in his banking and legal career and is so good with money. His eyes go a little wide when he sees the sums.

"What do you think?" Omar asks.

"I was thinking about Maimonides," Mr. Handell answers.

"Who?"

"A rabbi from the 12th century. He said there are eight levels of giving, each better than not giving at all. But the best and most noble are those times you give and they receive anonymously and you give to make someone self-sufficient."

Remember?

Omar looks at her, and she nods. "That's what we want, then," he says. "No one should ever know we've done it. We'll use what we need, factor in inflation and taxes and keep a fair cushion for emergencies, and the rest of every year's return can be donated anonymously to good charities. We'll leave the principal alone to generate money for the next year. Can you do this? Can you make this happen and keep it a secret?"

Mr. Handell nods. "With this much money you'll still have to actively manage how you invest and donate," he tells them. "That'll keep you busy. But I can make sure that no one knows it's you."

Another rock hit the wall. "I know you're in there, witch! I know you called the reporter! You just live to take things away from everybody else, don't you? You think it's all about you!"

Curled on the floor, trembling, she held the picture close.

Long ago.

The pain, the blood. The hospital and the doctor's face.

"I'm so sorry. It's a miscarriage. There's nothing we could have done."

Omar's hand in hers, the tears in his eyes. Her own words, choked with guilt.

"I'm sorry. I lost the baby. I'm sorry."

Her husband's lips, warm on her forehead.

"No. It's not your fault, Edith. I love you."

Forever.

"Witch!" the angry voice called from outside.

Omar standing, talking with her in their living room, and then mumbling something.

"I feel strange."

Catching him as he crumbles to the floor. Rushing to the phone, calling for help. After what seems an eternity, the ambulance, the wail of the sirens. Waiting, and then the doctor.

"It was a stroke, Mrs. MacCamey. Massive. There's nothing we could have done. I'm so sorry."

So sorry.

Seven

I suppose you know the rest, don't you? Betsy and her family pulled in, and Betsy exploded from the car, ran to Jip and seized his arm.

"Stop it!" she cried. "What are you doing?"

Her father was close behind, and her mother, and there was the look on Jip's face as he saw them, as he looked down at the stone in his hand. The air went out of him then, like a punctured balloon, the rage becoming something else. He slumped to the ground.

"I thought…." he managed, but said nothing more.

Sirens, coming fast. A patrol car with two officers, Hayes and Trujillo. They looked at the man sitting on the cold ground, at the girl and the second man beside her, at the fine car crunched against the snow in front of the old house. They surveyed the scene and approached.

"What's going on here?" Officer Hayes asked.

"He was throwing rocks at this house," answered Betty's father.

Recognition crossed the officer's face.

"Mr. Batton?"

Jip still sat motionless, only shaking his head and muttering quietly. Officer Hayes crouched beside him. Maybe he smelled the liquor on Jip's breath. Maybe he didn't need to.

"Come with me," he said, and they got Jip to his feet and over to the patrol car.

There were procedures now, for this sort of thing, even on Christmas Eve. A breathalyzer test, handcuffs, taking statements from Betsy and her father and her mother, and then Officer Trujillo stepped up to the Witch's front door and rang the bell.

A statement would be taken there too, just the facts Ma'am, but that's not important. What's important is that Betsy followed Officer Trujillo, and when he had finished for the time being with the old, shy woman, Betsy spoke to her from behind him.

"Are you all right, Mrs. MacCamey?"

Maybe it was the trembling hands, or the look on the old woman's face. Maybe it was the tone in Betsy's voice that told Officer Trujillo to get out of the way. All we do know is that the Witch stepped back and Betsy stepped inside.

"Let me help you clean it up," the girl said.

Bits of glass, so be careful. The Witch got a trash basket and Betsy began to pick the shards up, one by one with gloved hands (clever girl). Then she saw the pictures on the floor, including the one with the cracked frame. And as she put these back on the living room table Betsy asked what no adult would but any child might.

"Who's that?"

The old voice, the uncertain voice, the frightened voice.

"Omar. My husband."

"And this other picture. Is that you with him?"

One word. "Yes."

The old voice faltered then, broken like the bits of shattered glass that still lay here and there. How many decades of silence, held back by the dam of fear within and indifference outside? How long to mourn alone, afraid?

It broke. There and then, on Christmas Eve, on that oh holy night, it broke. A low sob, trembling as the Witch went to her knees, face in her hands, the shy girl, the strange girl, the young woman in love with a good young man, the mother to be who would never be, the widow at the fresh grave of her good man stolen by a stroke, all of it all of it all of it.

And Betsy, young but still wise somehow, moving forward to her friend and doing what had not been done for far too long. She wrapped her small arms around the Witch, and she held her close and let her weep the long overdue tears of grief and healing.

* * *

Mr. Handell parked and locked his car in front of the police station and then stepped inside. The officer on duty, Sergeant Jennison, looked up and greeted him, and they spoke for a few minutes. Then Officer Shryack was summoned and she took Mr. Handell back to the lock-up, where she opened the single occupied cell.

There within, sitting in what might have been lingering disbelief (and certainly a very bad hangover), was Jip Batton. He did not raise his eyes as Mr. Handell pulled up a chair.

"Good morning, Jip."

The gaze came up, then fell again.

"What do you want?"

"To talk. Do you have a lawyer?"

Jip just watched the floor.

"You may need one. In addition to the DWI, you broke the window of a private residence and some property inside. You can thank God that Betsy girl and her family showed up when they did and stopped you." Mr. Handell paused, letting his words sink in. "But you didn't hit Mrs. MacCamey, which is good. If you had, these would be much more serious charges and you and I wouldn't be having this pleasant little conversation. Do you understand?"

Jip nodded.

"No one knows why you did it," Mr. Handell said. "But it *is* what everyone is talking about, and that's put rather a damper on the Christmas festivities, needless to say. People are going to remember this for a very long time. Many in this town do like you, and some look up to you. They expect you to set a moral example. And so it's clear that everyone cares why you did it, everyone, that is, except for me. Because I honestly *don't* care, Jip. It would be easy for me to turn around and walk out of here and never talk to you or think about you again. That's something I want you to remember."

At this, a spasm of fear went through Jip Batton, something very deep, a thousand memories of a little boy watched always by his cold, distant parents, watched always with stern expectations to succeed and win regardless of the cost, a boy not permitted to play and be silly and messy as little boys should sometimes be. To be so ignored even as he was the center of attention, this child had learned, meant that he was not loved, that he was only a family trophy. Jip felt a deep spasm of shame now as another part of him saw who that child had become, and as he replayed again and again the memories of what he had done. But he realized also that the voice that came next was not his father, was not the distant man he had never really known. Instead, Mr. Handell's tone was surprisingly gentle.

"Fortunately, though, no one was hurt by your stunt, and we'd all like to be sure that you don't do anything like this ever again."

Jip looked up and kept his eyes raised this time. He opened his mouth to speak, to rationalize, to make everything all right with a clever explanation the way he had always done before, but then he saw Mr. Handell's gaze and the words died in his throat. Though perhaps not his father, this man would also not be swayed by smooth talk, by hollow reassurances. Stephen Handell saw truth, and could not be bought or sold.

"What now?" Jip asked instead.

"Well, I've posted your bail. It's not much, really; just what's appropriate for a drunken lout who drove when he shouldn't have and broke an old woman's window. After the judge or jury decides what to do about your DWI, Mrs. MacCamey will have to choose whether or not to press charges, so be glad this isn't a serious felony. At the very least I think you owe her a sincere, public apology and a new window. You also need to leave her alone. But I will answer your question with a question: What now? Who do you choose to be, Jip Batton?"

Jip brought a hand up and rubbed his brow.

"I don't know," he said, and realized as he did that it was the first time he had spoken his own deepest truth in many years, the words and feelings unfamiliar. "I thought I did, but I don't."

"Fair enough, and honest. Humility is a good start, if you can hang on to it. But keep in mind that it's not enough to simply make a promise, Jip. You need to actually do what you say you will, to really think about others. You need to get help if you find that you can't. You need that humility." Mr. Handell watched him closely, then added, "If you do decide to change, there might be hope. But there is another question also."

"Oh?" asked Jip Batton.

"It is the Hanukkah season, and my wife and I are having our usual Hanukkah and Christmas dinner gathering with some friends. You are welcome to come, Jip, and we would all be pleased if you joined us."

So the first white Christmas in a generation came to an end in the little town. There would never be another one like it, everyone agreed, never again quite so many lights downtown or displays in every window. Instead the holidays that followed became quieter, gentler, with

simpler gatherings and songs that filled the
night. And while there were certainly still trees
and tinsel and presents, while Santa still arrived
and laughed his jolly "Ho! Ho! Ho!," with
Hanukkah candles still lit in honor of the
ancient ceremony, now it all meant more than it
had.

The Witch became something different too.
She was still little seen, but the curtains to her
windows were now commonly drawn open
during the day and instead of being an object of
fear or scorn she became a figure of love in the
neighborhood and the community. When she
did go out to the store or to visit a friend or to
Mr. Handell's office or even to the cemetery,
people did not turn away but instead might
greet her with a smile and a quiet hello,
expecting nothing more in return. Mothers and
fathers now told their children to approach her,
and she always smiled at these and talked gently
with them, seeing more than anyone suspected.
Every autumn some of the local teenagers
would come to her house and clean up the
inevitable brush in her yard, and if she still
stayed inside, this was fine, because there would

always be fresh cookies and bottles of water and they knew that the nice Mr. Handell would appear when they were through with an envelope containing thank you notes and fresh twenty-dollar bills to share, which came to be called "Betsy Bucks" and which were considered a great honor.

And of course holidays still came and went, every year marked by the reading of Torah at Pesach, sunrise worship on Easter Sunday, the *'iftār* meal to break the fast after sunset during Ramadan. People gathered to observe Kwanzaa or Vijayadashami, Diwali or Vesak, or perhaps the six Gahambar festivals and Naw Rúz, the Dragon Boat Festival or Shinkō-sai Procession, and many more, including the sacred days and celebrations of indigenous peoples everywhere, every faith and culture of humanity. For these are the seasons of Peace on Earth and goodwill towards all, of kindness, charity and forgiveness, and most of all a time to remember that what you may see of any other person is never the whole of them, or even of you yourself.

Let it be compassion, therefore, and not the hunger for fame, that guides your charity, on this holiday and every other day.

Lump of Coal

All right, I admit it. I was up late on Christmas Eve. But trust me, it's not because I'm naughty. I had, in fact, intended to go to bed, to dream of sugarplums and so forth, but sleep would not come. I don't know why, really. I don't get insomnia much and I don't drink coffee after 3pm, and I never drink more than a glass of wine at any one time.

So anyway, there I was, up late on Christmas Eve, which you're just not supposed to do. And suddenly, up on the rooftop, there came the sound of hoofs, of feet, followed by motion in the chimney. A bag dropped into my fireplace, followed by a pair of black boots, and then a man far too large to fit through so small a passage. But he did it somehow, all dressed in red, with white fluffy fringes and a thick belt.

Yeah, you know who he is.

Santa Claus? I blinked.

Santa Claus.

He straightened, dusted himself off, stepped from the fireplace, and saw me. "Ho!" he cried, his voice deep and jolly, exactly as you'd expect. "What's this?"

"Just me," I answered.

"Up so late?" he asked. "This is highly unusual." He reached into his pocket and produced a long list. "Says here you've been nice, and I know about these things. So why aren't you in bed dreaming happy dreams?"

"Don't know," I told him, and I repeated for him what I just told you, about my lack of insomnia and lack of caffeine and alcohol. "Maybe I'm just stressed about the holiday."

"Tell me about it," Santa said. He sat down on the edge of the fireplace and helped himself to a cookie. "The whole week before Christmas, I'm a wreck. Half the time, Mrs. Claus threatens to leave me and move in with her sister. Do you have any idea how hard it is to get flight clearance for every country on Earth, even if they know you're coming?"

I shook my head. "You want anything to wash down those cookies?" I asked.

"Nog me," he answered. I handed him the mug, and he took a drink and smiled. I thought about hyperglycemia as he spoke again. "But enough about me," he said. "You're up, so technically, no presents for you."

"None?"

"Nope. Sorry. It's the rule. Paragraph something-something in the manual. I forget the exact number, but you can take my word for it."

I nodded. If you can't trust Santa…. But still, a shame, that.

"Don't get me wrong," he added. "If it was up to me, I would." He glanced at his list again. "You've been pretty good this year. Not perfect, mind you, but who ever is? The stories I could tell you!" I looked over at him as he ate the next cookie and followed this with some more eggnog. "These cookies are good," he told me. "Bake them yourself?"

"No. Trust me, you don't want to eat *my* cooking."

His eyes twinkled and he laughed his hearty *Ho Ho Ho!* But then he looked at me more seriously. "I should get going," he said. "I've still got to cover California and the West Coast, and Central and South America always have a lot of good kids. Sorry about the no presents thing. I never like to leave anyone without at least something for Christmas."

I considered this. I don't really need more stuff; most people don't, when you get right down to it. Presents are more about giving and receiving than having, and way too many of them just wind up in the landfill.

"How about a favor, then?" I asked.

"A favor?"

I looked at his bag of toys. "Yeah."

"What did you have in mind? Nothing illegal, I hope. Ever since that whole Enchilada Affair my accountant says I have to be careful."

"No, no, nothing like that. I just thought that if you can't give me anything, you're going to have some spare toys, yes?"

Santa nodded. "Makes it hard on the reindeer," he said. "Last year Prancer tore a ligament and was out for six weeks. The Reindeer Union filed a complaint with OSHA."

"Well, then, could you just give my toys to someone else?"

His nose wiggled and his mustache with it, scattering cookie crumbs.

"Hm. Never thought of that. Who do you have in mind?"

"Who's next to get a lump of coal?"

He checked his list twice and gave me some names.

"Well, give my toys to them," I told him.

"This is highly irregular," he said. "Sort of defeats the purpose of the naughty/nice reward for good behavior concept, doesn't it? Where's the moral lesson if naughty kids get toys?"

"I don't know," I answered. "But where's the moral lesson in punishment without an explanation? You show up, leave the coal, and are gone. Maybe the naughty children need the gifts and the love from them most of all."

He chuckled now, a full Santa jelly-belly chuckle. "God, you sound like the Dalai Lama," he said, and then the twinkle came back into his eye. "All right, it's a deal. It'll make the accountants squirm, but that'll be good for them. Your toys for the naughty children, and I'll leave them a note telling them why. Maybe it'll help them be nice next year."

"It's worth a try."

Santa nodded and turned for the chimney. Then he reached into his bag, pulled something out, and tossed it to me. "Hate to give you this," he told me, "but it's the regulation."

I nodded, and as he disappeared up the chimney, I opened my hand.

A single lump of coal lay there.

I still have that lump, you know, kept close by my bed every Christmas Eve. It is the finest gift I have ever received, and I hope every year for another one.

Teddy Bear

I was sleeping when he came to me, in that place between dreams and reality where you don't know what is and what is not, what matters. He bore the marks of age, the experience of a thousand adventures in his worn fur, the missing buttons of his eyes, the places where my mother had patiently stitched up the holes in his skin. I recognized him, knew him instantly, my old and dear friend. I remembered another dream from long ago, a nightmare of losing him and then awakening to find him there beside me, always loyal. I remembered the many years of childhood, of adolescence, even adulthood, when things and people change, when the world changes from one uncertainty into the greater one of growing up. Always there, always patient and waiting for me, love in his cloth skin and foam stuffing, eternal.

He called my name. I answered.

"Come," he said.

He led me not just through places but also through times, through ages. We stopped then, staring at a child, and he asked me, "Do you remember this?"

"I do," I said.

"What do you remember?"

"I was alone."

He regarded me with the eyes that were not there and yet that saw through me.

"Were you?"

The child looked back at both of us, and I answered.

"No. You were there."

He smiled, though he had no jaw, only that tiny red tongue beneath his nose. The nose protects the hair, that one bit of his fur still fresh. I remember how he felt, on that Christmas Eve when I opened the package, tearing away the bright paper to find the box, and him within.

Teddy. Teddy the bear.

My friend.

"Come," he said again.

We passed through time, through places that were unfamiliar. I held to him, trusting him. At last we stopped.

"Do you see?" he asked.

There was a little boy there, one I did not know. He held a bear, new and fresh, a bright ribbon around its neck, one different and yet familiar from my memory. The boy was smiling, a toothless child's smile, the bear close.

"Do you see?" Teddy asked again.

The boy grew. His bear grew with him, and they played in an unfamiliar home, an unfamiliar place. But they were together.

"I don't understand," I said. "Who is he?"

Teddy didn't answer.

There was a little girl now, with freckles and pigtails, and she too held a bear. This bear had a bow on its head, a pink bow, but it was still the same bear, the same as Teddy. The little girl drank imaginary tea with her bear, talking with it, sharing secrets.

Another child. Another bear. Another. Another. Each unique and yet the same, passing before me, and Teddy said nothing.

I watched.

The children changed now. They grew older, boys becoming young men, girls becoming young women, others simply becoming who they really were. The bears were relegated to boxes, lost in closets.

"Who are they?" I asked again.

"You know them," Teddy answered.

Lives passed. A young man, dressed for his wedding day. A young woman, holding her first child. Work. Joy. Pain. Arguments and celebrations and disappointments. One man now, in the hospital, his eyes looking up into eternity as he breathed his last. Another embracing his wife, having no words for a sorrow. Another celebrating, surrounded by his own children, happy. A mother holding her son close.

All of these passed before me.

And one man then, finding the box in the attic, his expression as he saw the bear within. A wistful smile, perhaps a memory evoked. Holding the old bear as he showed it to his children.

"Do you know who this is?" he asked them.

"No, Papa."

"This is Bobbins the bear. Your grandma gave him to me when I was little, a long time ago."

Teddy looked at me.

"Do you know who I am?" he asked me.

"Teddy," I said. "You are my old and dear friend."

"Yes," he said. "And who are they, these others, these people?"

"Strangers," I answered.

"No."

"I don't understand," I said. "I don't know them."

"Don't you?" Teddy asked. "Each of you shared one of us. There are thousands of Teddys, millions of bears in all shapes and sizes and colors. Each of you held us and felt our love. But more than this each of you, and the billions beyond, are alive, are part of the greater family of humanity. You share so much more than you differ, and yet you forget this when you look at each other and see a stranger, when you retreat into distrust, fear, tribalism. And that is why we Teddy Bears are here, my friend. We are with you through all those things you feel you can never share. We are the confidants who will never betray your trust. But more than this we Teddy Bears, together, all of us, are here to remind you that you are not alone. For every thought or fear or joy you have, there is another person somewhere, holding another bear, who has one likewise. Remember that when you meet a stranger you are meeting a part of yourself. That is what it means to be human."

I watched him and he watched me back, through the lost button eyes that would forever see so deeply. And I spoke the truth that we both knew.

"You are my friend," I said.

"Always," he answered, and I held him close.

CPSIA information can be obtained
at www.ICGtesting.com
Printed in the USA
BVHW041009211221
624502BV00016B/701